surf
1978

For my papa—
the eternal source of
joy and happiness

For my mama—
the eternal source of
love and wisdom

About This Book • The illustrations for this book were created using pen, ink, gouache, and Photoshop. The text was set in Nicolas Cochin Black Regular, and the display type is P22 Stanyan Bold. • Text and illustrations copyright © 2019 by Elina Ellis • Cover illustration copyright © 2019 by Elina Ellis. Cover design by Christine Kettner and Véronique Lefèvre Sweet. • Cover copyright © 2019 by Hachette Book Group, Inc. • Hachette Book Group supports the right to free expression and the value of copyright. The purpose of copyright is to encourage writers and artists to produce the creative works that enrich our culture. The scanning, uploading, and distribution of this book without permission is a theft of the author's intellectual property. If you would like permission to use material from the book (other than for review purposes), please contact permissions@hbgusa.com. Thank you for your support of the author's rights. • Little, Brown and Company, Hachette Book Group, 1290 Avenue of the Americas, New York, NY 10104 • Visit us at LBYR.com

Originally published as *The Truth About Old People* in 2019 by Pan Macmillan in the United Kingdom • First U.S. Edition: September 2019 • Little, Brown and Company is a division of Hachette Book Group, Inc. • The Little, Brown name and logo are trademarks of Hachette Book Group, Inc. • The publisher is not responsible for websites (or their content) that are not owned by the publisher.

Library of Congress Cataloging-in-Publication Data • Names: Ellis, Elina, author, illustrator. • Title: The truth about grandparents / by Elina Ellis. • Other titles: Truth about old people • Description: First U.S. edition. | New York ; Boston : Little, Brown Books for Young Readers, 2019. | "Originally published as The Truth About Old People in 2019 by Pan Macmillan in the United Kingdom." | Summary: A child relates strange things that might be heard about grandparents, but concludes that they are amazing. • Identifiers: LCCN 2018058153 | ISBN 9780316424721 (hardcover) | ISBN 9780316424684 (ebook) | ISBN 9780316424714 (library edition ebook) • Subjects: | CYAC: Grandparents—Fiction. | Old age—Fiction. • Classification: LCC PZ7. E4715 Tru 2019 | DDC [E]—dc23 • LC record available at https://lccn. loc.gov/2018058153 • ISBNs: 978-0-316-42472-1 (hardcover), 978-0-316-42468-4 (ebook), 978-0-316-42470-7 (ebook), 978-0-316-42467-7 (ebook)

PRINTED IN CHINA BY WKT. CO.

10 9 8 7 6 5 4 3 2 1

The TRUTH About GRANDPARENTS

Elina Ellis

LB

Little, Brown and Company ★ New York Boston

My grandparents are *really* old.

They have wrinkly faces,
a little bit of hair, and funny teeth.

I've been hearing lots of strange
things about old people.

Some people say they are

NOT MUCH FUN.

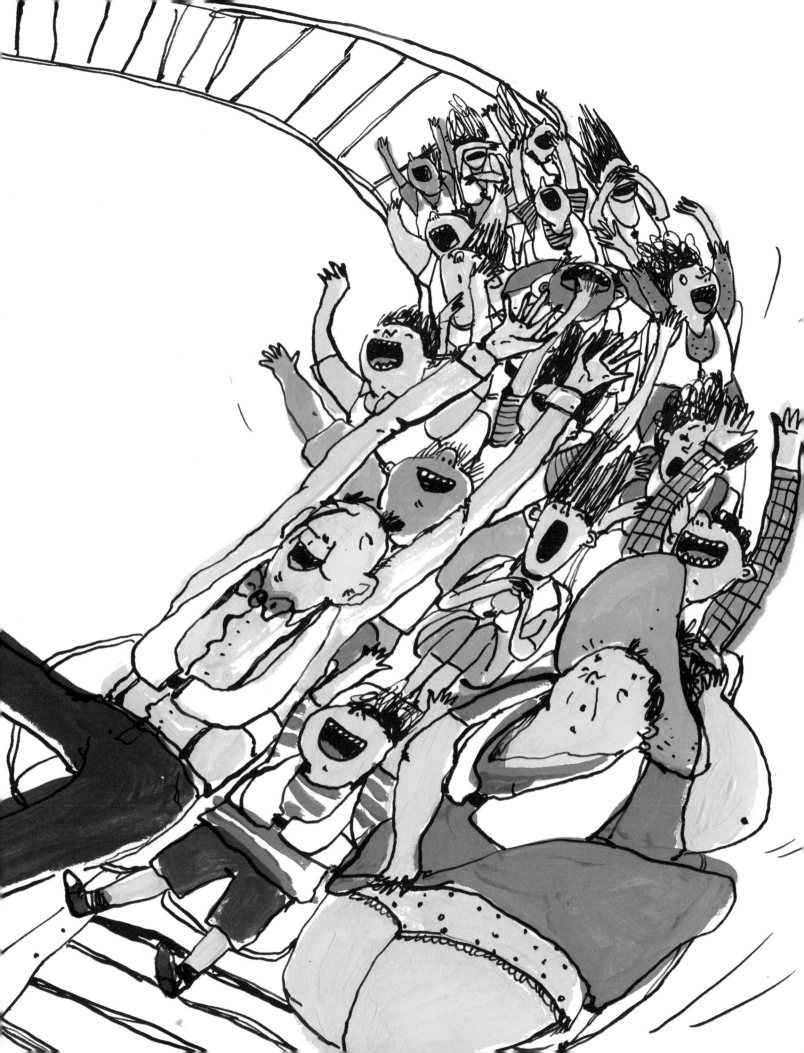

They say that grandparents are

SLOW...

and

CLUMSY . . .

and

NOT BENDY.

Someone told me grandparents are

SCARED

of new things…

THEY

DON'T

EVER

DANCE...

and they
definitely don't care for

ROMANCE.

They say that grandparents are

QUIET...

and grandparents are

NOT AT ALL
ADVENTUROUS.

But I know the
truth about grandparents.

Grandparents are . . .

AMA

ZING!